Adventure to
Adelie Land

PRICE STERN SLOAN
Published by the Penguin Group
Penguin Group (USA) Inc., 375 Hudson Street, New York, New York 10014, USA
Penguin Group (Canada), 90 Eglinton Avenue East, Suite 700, Toronto, Ontario M4P 2Y3, Canada
(a division of Pearson Penguin Canada Inc.)
Penguin Books Ltd., 80 Strand, London WC2R 0RL, England
Penguin Group Ireland, 25 St. Stephen's Green, Dublin 2, Ireland
(a division of Penguin Books Ltd.)
Penguin Group (Australia), 250 Camberwell Road, Camberwell, Victoria 3124, Australia
(a division of Pearson Australia Group Pty. Ltd.)
Penguin Books India Pvt. Ltd., 11 Community Centre, Panchsheel Park, New Delhi—110 017, India
Penguin Group (NZ), 67 Apollo Drive, Rosedale, Auckland 0632, New Zealand
(a division of Pearson New Zealand Ltd.)
Penguin Books (South Africa) (Pty.) Ltd., 24 Sturdee Avenue,
Rosebank, Johannesburg 2196, South Africa

Penguin Books Ltd., Registered Offices: 80 Strand, London WC2R 0RL, England

ISBN 978-0-8431-9817-1   10 9 8 7 6 5 4 3 2

HAPPY FEET TWO™

Adventure to Adelie Land

by Sophia Kelly
illustrated by Nick O'Sullivan

PSS!
PRICE STERN SLOAN
An Imprint of Penguin Group (USA) Inc.

This is Mumble.

Mumble loves to dance.

This is Gloria.

Gloria loves to sing.

Mumble and Gloria live in
Emperor Land.

They have a son, Erik.

Erik is very little and very shy.

Sometimes, Erik feels like he

does not belong in Emperor Land.

He cannot dance like

the other Emperor penguins.

Mumble tells Erik

he knows how that feels.

Mumble could not sing

when he was a baby penguin.

But he was brave and danced!

Erik does not think he can

be as brave as his dad.

This is Ramon.

Ramon is from Adelie Land.

Ramon tells Erik about
Adelie Land, where you can
be who you want to be.

Erik has an idea.

He will go to Adelie Land

with Ramon!

This is Bo and Atticus.

They are Erik's friends.

Bo and Atticus want to go to
Adelie Land with Erik and Ramon.

Erik, Bo, and Atticus help Ramon

jump into the ocean.

Ramon is catching fish

to eat on the trip to Adelie Land.

Erik thinks Ramon is very brave.

Jumping into the ocean

must be scary!

Mumble is on his way
to Adelie Land to find
Erik, Bo, and Atticus.

Mumble wants to bring

the baby penguins

home to Emperor Land.

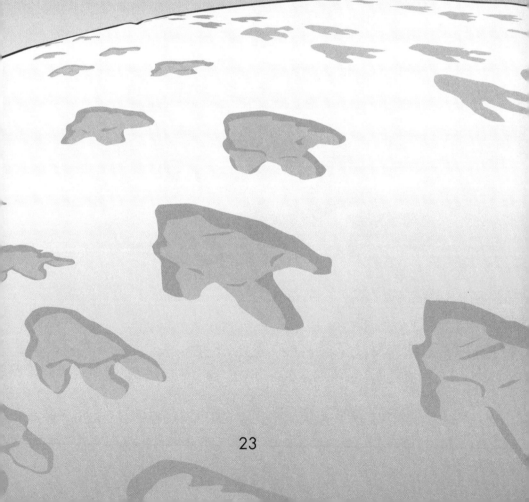

Ramon, Erik, Bo, and Atticus
arrive in Adelie Land.
They meet Sven.

Sven can fly!

Erik thinks Sven is very brave.

Flying high above must be scary!

Mumble arrives in Adelie Land.

He finds Erik, Atticus, and Bo!

It is time for Mumble and
the baby penguins to go home
to Emperor Land.

On their way back to
Emperor Land, Erik thinks
his dad is very brave.

Mumble swims faster than
a Leopard seal who is
chasing him!

Erik thinks his friends

are brave, too.

Bo and Atticus jump

on an Elephant seal

who is blocking their path!

Back in Emperor Land,

Erik is brave—he dances.

He does belong in

Emperor Land after all!